Mr Buzz the Beeman

by ALLAN AHLBERG

with pictures by

FAITH JAQUES

PUFFIN BOOKS

Published by the Penguin Group
Penguin Books Ltd, 80 Strand, London, WC2R 0RL, England
Penguin Group (USA), Inc., 375 Hudson Street, New York, New York 10014, USA
Penguin Books Australia Ltd, 250 Camberwell Road, Camberwell, Victoria 3124, Australia
Penguin Books Canada Ltd, 10 Alcorn Avenue, Toronto, Ontario, Canada M4V 3B2
Penguin Books India (P) Ltd, 11 Community Centre, Panchsheel Park, New Delhi – 110 017, India
Penguin Group (NZ), cnr Airborne and Rosedale Roads, Albany, Auckland 1310, New Zealand
Penguin Books (South Africa) (Pty) Ltd, 24 Sturdee Avenue, Rosebank 2196, South Africa

Penguin Books Ltd, Registered Offices: 80 Strand, London WC2R 0RL, England

puffinbooks.com

First published by Viking 1981
Published in Puffin Books 1981
29 30 28

Educational Advisory Editor: Brian Thompson

Set in Century Schoolbook by Filmtype Services Limited, Scarborough
Manufactured in China

ISBN-13 : 978-0-14031-244-7

There was once a beeman
named Mr Buzz.
Mr Buzz lived in a cottage
with his wife and children.
They had a cow, a cat, two canaries,
three goldfish, five bee-hives –

and a hundred-and-fifty thousand bees!

Every day the bees worked hard.
They flew from flower to flower.
They took nectar back to the hives
and made the honey.
They were as busy as bees.
Every day Mr Buzz and his family
worked hard too.
Mr Buzz took the honey from the hives
Mrs Buzz put it into the honey-pots.
Master Buzz made labels
for the honey-pots.
Miss Buzz stuck them on.

One morning Mr Buzz was working in the garden.
He was making a new bee-hive.
Suddenly he saw a terrible thing.
Some of the bees were in a swarm – and they were flying away!

When bees fly off in a swarm,
they almost never come back.
Mr Buzz knew this.
"The bees are buzzing off!" he cried.
So then Mr Buzz and his family
put on their bee-hats
and their bee-gloves,
picked up a bee-basket –
and went chasing after the bees.

The bees flew down the road.
A postman was riding by on his bike.
"The bees are buzzing off!"
cried Mr Buzz.
"The little rascals," the postman said.
"I will help you catch them!"

The bees flew over a farmer's field,
with Mr Buzz and his family,
and the postman on his bike
all chasing after.

The farmer and his dog
were in the field.
"The bees are buzzing off!"
cried Mr Buzz.

"The little scamps," the farmer said.
"I will help you catch them!"
The bees flew by the river,
with Mr Buzz and his family,
and the postman on his bike,

and the farmer with his dog
all chasing after.

A fisherman with his rod and line
was sitting on the bank.
"The bees are buzzing off!"
cried Mr Buzz.
"The little devils," the fisherman said.
"I will help you catch them!"

The bees flew past the village school,
with Mr Buzz and his family,
and the postman on his bike,
and the farmer with his dog,
and the fisherman with his rod and line
all chasing after.

The teacher and the children
were in the playground.
"The bees are buzzing off!"
cried Mr Buzz.
"The little beasts," the teacher said.
"We will help you catch them!"

The bees flew by the village church,
with Mr Buzz and his family,
and the postman on his bike,
and the farmer with his dog,
and the fisherman with his rod and line,
and the teacher and the children
from the school
all chasing after.

A wedding group was standing
on the steps.
"The bees are buzzing off!"
cried Mr Buzz.
"The little scallywags," the bride said.
"We will help you catch them!"

The bees flew *up* the road,
with Mr Buzz and his family,
and the postman on his bike,
and the farmer with his dog,
and the fisherman with his rod and line,
and the teacher and the children
from the school,

and the bride and groom,
and wedding guests and bridesmaids
from the church
all chasing after.

Suddenly Mr Buzz saw where the bees were going.
"Those bees are not buzzing off!" he cried.
"They are buzzing back again!"
And so they were –
straight back into the new hive that Mr Buzz had made.

Then everyone said,
"The little rascals!"
"The little scamps!"
"The little devils!"
"The little beasts!"
"The little scallywags!"

The little scamps!
The little rascals!
They are uzzing back again!

After that Mr Buzz and his family,
and the postman on his bike,
and the farmer with his dog,
and the fisherman with his rod and line,
and the teacher and the children
from the school,
and the bride and groom,

and wedding guests and bridesmaids
from the church –
all sat down in the garden
and had honey for tea.
"Our bees made this," said Mr Buzz
as he passed the honey-pots around.
And everyone said . . .

. . . "The little angels!"

The little angels!
The little angels!

The End